Gabrielle Bourne

GHOST HORSE
MYSTERY

by DJ Arneson and Tony Tallarico

Watermill Press

GHOST HORSE
MYSTERY

CONTENTS

Phantom Footsteps

Clump, clump, clump.

The phantom footsteps were back.

The first time we heard the noise was last week when we were cleaning out the actor's dressing room here in the old opera house. Dell's dad, who just happens to be the mayor of Montville, hired our whole club, all five of us, to clean up the opera house. "It's an eyesore," he said. Well, maybe it looks like an eyesore to a grownup, but it sure doesn't look that way to me. It's kind of neat, I think.

The opera house looks just like it did when they closed it during the Second World War. My dad told me how he used to come down here with Gram and Gramps to see plays and things. He was just a kid then, so this place must be really old.

Anyway, there's a table and some chairs on the stage that were part of the last play they gave. I looked at a couple of the magazines on the table. They were props. They were dated 1942. One's a *Saturday Evening Post* and the other doesn't have a cover. They're both full of old-fashioned pictures and things. It proves how long this place has been empty.

There was a Coca-Cola ad in the *Saturday Evening Post* magazine. I didn't know they had Coke when my dad was a kid, but I guess they did because it's right there in that magazine on the table.

Sandy was the first one to hear the phantom footsteps. She was back in the dressing room that's next to the stage. When she tried to turn on the lights a fuse blew out. It got as dark as the inside of a gunny sack in here.

It was just before everybody started yelling "turn on the lights" when she heard the footsteps.

Tyler fixed the lights in a minute. He's about the smartest one of us for that kind of thing. When the lights came on, Sandy came streaking out of that dressing room like it was on fire.

"There's something in there!" she hollered.

We all thought she meant a mouse or a bat or something like that. There were only the five of us in the opera house and Sandy was the only one in the dressing room, so what else could it be?

Anyway, when she screamed there was something in there, we listened. Anybody would. It's creepy enough in this old place with all the lights on and everybody talking. Imagine what it's like in the dark.

We laughed at first. Tyler said she was hearing things.

Then Sandy said, "That's what I said. I did hear something in there."

That made us laugh all the more. But I noticed it was the kind of nervous laugh you laugh when you're not sure about things.

"What kind of things?" Tyler asked.

He's that way. Precise, if you know what I mean. Like when you say you saw something, he'll ask you what color it was and how fast it was going and things like that. I have to admit he's good to have around, though, because otherwise this club would fall apart. If you've ever tried to get a club going, you know what I mean. It's like trying to organize your brothers and sisters. Or a bunch of Cub Scouts. People are like ants, I guess. They all sort of go their own way. That's the way it is with our club, anyway. That's why Tyler's a good guy to have around.

"I don't know what kind of things," Sandy

told him. "If I knew what it was, I would have told you."

The conversation was really getting nowhere. Tyler was trying to be scientific and Sandy didn't have anything scientific to tell him.

So then Dell made his famous suggestion.

"Let's go and see," he said.

That put an end to the discussion right away.

"All right!" I said. It sounded like a pretty good idea to me. It was better than standing around.

I should have kept my mouth shut. Everybody turned to me and said, "O.k., Andy, you go first." That's when the idea didn't look so good anymore. All of a sudden this old opera house started looking like something out of a monster movie.

It really does. There are thick maroon curtains hanging on both sides of the stage that are covered with dust and cobwebs. Then there's the ceiling, which is full of little plaster statues of angels and a bunch of stars and moons. And all around the auditorium, which is full of all these old, dusty seats, are a bunch of statues of Greeks wearing togas. And to make matters worse, right over the middle of the stage near the ceiling is a big circle with two huge heads in it with one guy laughing and the other guy crying. I've seen that somewhere before, but I don't remember where. A book, I think.

Then there's the stage. Like I said, it's still got a sofa and some chairs and a table on it like somebody's old-fashioned living room. The walls are made out of canvas and they're painted to look like a room. There's even a bird painted on a tree outside a painted window that keeps looking in at you like it was real and you're not.

On the left side of the stage is the dressing room. Well, you can see why I wasn't too interested in going back. But everybody was waiting for me, so I did.

I took the broom I had been sweeping the stage with and held it up like a samurai sword with two hands.

"O.k.," I said. "I'll go first, but you guys have to come with me."

I started across the stage toward the dressing room really slowly so the others could catch up. I don't mind being a hero as long as there are enough witnesses around. That way you can look brave and the witnesses don't know they're really backing you up. Who wants to be a hero all by himself? Not me.

I poked the broom into the dressing room and wagged the end around. I didn't feel it hit anything, so I went in. I thought the others were right behind me, so it really wasn't as bad as it sounds. The trouble was they were still out on the stage and I didn't know it.

It was dark in the dressing room.

"It's dark in here," I said. "I thought you fixed the lights, Tyler."

All I needed was to get trapped inside a pitch dark room about as big as a closet that nobody has been in since before television was invented.

Then I heard the footsteps.

Clump. Clump. Clump.

"Be quiet, you guys," I said. I still thought everybody was right behind me or I'd have been out of there faster than Roadrunner on Saturday morning, which is what day it was.

Clump. Clump. Clump.

I never heard anything like that noise before in my life. I got so cold that I thought somebody had put on the air conditioning. It was like a refrigerator in that little dark room. I was just wearing a t-shirt and a pair of shorts anyway and

I started to freeze. Goose bumps started popping up on my arms like the bumps on a basketball. I felt a cold wind on my neck, which I thought was Sandy breathing on it.

"Cut that out, Sandy," I said. But nobody answered because they heard the noise, too. They just took off, leaving me there holding a stupid broom for protection. When I turned around and nobody was there, that's when I took off, too.

We talked about the noise when we got across the street to Walgreen's. We sat in our usual booth in the back and split a couple of diet Pepsis. That's so Tricia could have some, too. Her parents don't let her drink or eat anything with sugar in it. Her dad runs a health food store.

"Who heard it?" Tyler asked.

Everybody looked at him like he just moved to town.

"What do you mean, who?" Sandy said. "We all did. Why do you think we ran all the way down here—to try out for the Olympics or something?"

"I was just taking a sample," Tyler said. "I want to know exactly who heard it."

Everybody sighed except Tyler. We wanted to talk about the clumping noise and he wanted to make some kind of statistics out of it.

"Sandy heard it," I said. "And I heard it and Dell heard it and Tricia heard it. That's four out of five. And if you heard it that makes it 100 percent. How's that for statistics?"

Everybody grinned except Tyler. I wasn't putting him down, but sometimes he's just too much.

"What exactly did you hear?"

That did it.

"Oh, come on, Tyler," Tricia said. "We all heard a *clump, clump, clump* and you know it. Who knows what it was? That's why we're here—to figure it out. Now let's talk about it instead of analyzing everything. What fun is that?"

Coming from Tricia, that was a mouthful.

Well, the whole thing was we couldn't figure out what the noise was. And that was last week. So now we're back in the opera house to find out. This time we brought flashlights.

"Shhh," Tyler whispered. "I'm going to turn on the lights."

It was ten times quieter in there this week than last week.

"I hear them," I said.

Sandy, Tyler, Tricia and Dell were right behind me this time. I don't know why I always get stuck being in the lead when we do stuff like this. I'm getting sick of it.

Clump. Clump. Clump. Clump.

The clumping sound was coming from the dressing room again. Tyler flicked on the lights. The clumping stopped.

We went back to Walgreen's to figure out a different strategy.

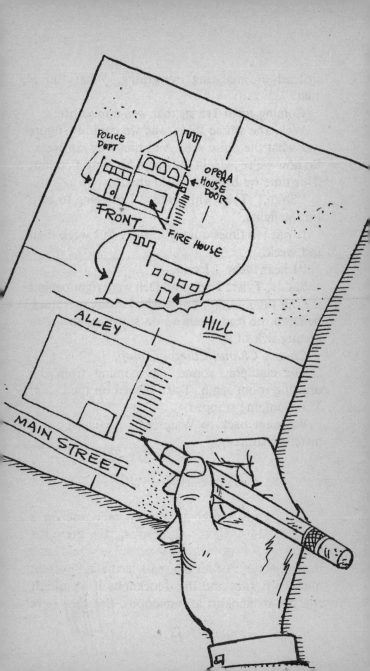

The Noise in the
Dressing Room

Tyler drew a map of the opera house on a napkin. He drew the floor plan. He drew the front view. He drew the side view. He would have drawn pictures of all the seats in the auditorium and the statues and the doorknobs if we didn't run out of napkins at our booth. But they were pretty good pictures, so nobody complained.

The opera house is on the top floor of the fire department and police department. It's in a big, old building on the hill on Main Street.

To get into the opera house you have to go up the stairs from the fire hall or through the regular entrance on the side that's part way up the hill. The side is locked, but Dell's dad gave us the keys.

"The only other way anything could get inside is through the alley door," Tyler said. He was admiring his own drawings.

"It's locked," Dell said.

"I know," Tyler replied. "The only way that isn't locked is up the stairs in the back of the fire hall."

"If that's how it got in, somebody would have seen it," Tricia said.

Nobody knew what the "it" was. That was the mystery.

"Precisely," Tyler answered. He was chewing on the eraser of his pencil.

"Let's ask the firemen if they saw anything go up there," I suggested.

"My dad said we're not supposed to bother the firemen," Dell said.

"There's only Sparky," Sandy said. "All the rest are volunteers. They only come around here for meetings or when there's a fire."

"We could start a fire. . ."

Tyler bit off the end of his pencil and nearly

swallowed the eraser. "Start a fire?" he gulped.

I was only kidding, but Tyler is so serious he hardly ever gets my jokes.

"I was only kidding," I said.

Tyler spit the end of the pencil into a napkin and rolled it into a neat little ball that he dropped into his pocket. You figure out why. Nobody else can.

"Well, let's ask Sparky if he saw anything go up the stairs," Tricia said.

We all agreed that would be the best way to get the mystery figured out in a hurry. Sparky wasn't really a fireman. He's more like a custodian.

"You claim you hear a thumpin' thumpin' thumpin' up there, eh?" Sparky asked. We woke him up from his nap that he takes every afternoon in his chair at the back of the firehouse. It's near the stairs.

Sandy shook her head. She was the first one to hear the noise, so she was the authority.

"No," she said. "It's not a thumpin' thumpin' thumpin'. It's a *thump, thump, thump.*"

Sparky scratched his head. "What's the difference?" he asked.

"A *thump* is a noise," Sandy answered, "like there's something up there. A thumpin's just a word."

Sparky leaned back in his chair. I don't think he understood the difference.

"Well, whatever it is, I ain't seen nothing go up or down these stairs for 20 years except for you kids. Now get on with your cleanin' if that's what you're doin' and let me get a nap in before it's time for my evening snooze.''

We weren't getting any closer to the solution to the mystery than we were before. We went up the stairs. This time we listened every step of the way.

The auditorium was empty, which was what we expected. But there was a light on in the dressing room. We didn't expect that.

''I thought the dressing room lights didn't work,'' Sandy said. She was looking at Tyler.

''I didn't say they didn't work,'' Tyler said. ''You did. You were the one in there when the fuses burned out.''

''Don't blame me for burning out the fuses,'' Sandy said. She looked kind of upset.

''I didn't. I just said. . .''

''Ssssshhhhh!''

Everybody turned to Tricia. Her head was cocked to one side like a robin listening for worms on a wet lawn.

''What?'' Dell asked. He was getting nervous.

''Sh!''

The place was eerier than usual. There's a smell in the old opera house that always reminds you of tombs and things like that. It smells like wet dust.

We were all staring at the light coming out of the open dressing room door. It was so quiet you could hear the pigeons walking around on the roof.

''Eeeeeeeee!''

That wasn't pigeons. Whatever it was wasn't very loud, but it was loud enough to give us all goose bumps this time. I felt rougher than a piece of sandpaper.

"It's coming from the dressing room," Tyler said. He took a step toward the open door.

Then a big grin cut across his face like he just remembered a joke or something. "It's only steam from the radiator, you guys," he laughed. He walked toward the door like there wasn't anything mysterious going on at all.

"In the middle of *July*?"

Tricia's question hit old Tyler like a sack of wet sand. He stopped in the middle of a step and didn't move a muscle.

"Eeeeeee!"

The noise was really loud this time. We all stood as still as stones. Poor old Tyler was stuck halfway to the open door.

The light in the doorway flickered a couple of times like a candle going out and then it was gone. We stood there like fireplugs or something. Nobody dared to move.

"We can't stand here all day," Sandy said.

That kind of broke the tension. I turned on my flashlight. With the light in the dressing room gone, it was more like night than day in there.

I pointed the beam at the stage. The curtain was open as usual. There was nothing any different than it was when we left about an hour ago. Except I knew something was.

The Footprint in
the Dust

"You guys stay close behind me this time," I said. I wasn't going to get left in the dark all by myself like before.

"We're right behind you," Tyler said.

"Well, stay there," I said. I started down the aisle. I don't know why I was acting so brave. All

I had this time was a flashlight, which isn't nearly as good as a broom. And a broom is worthless. I should know.

The rows of seats in the auditorium in front of the stage have a kind of spooky look. Sometimes you get the idea that there are people in them, just the way there used to be when the opera house was in use.

I walked down the aisle as slowly as I could so none of the others would have an excuse for falling behind. The trouble was, the slower I went, the more it seemed like there were people in the seats. I don't know which was worse, being all by myself or being surrounded by all those shadowy seats.

I kept the flashlight beam pointed straight ahead.

"We could use some more light in here," I said.

"I'll go back and try the switch," Dell said.

"No way," I said. "You stay with us just in case." I didn't know in case what, but I didn't want to take any chances.

"I'll see if I can turn on some more lights when we get to the stage," Tyler said.

That wasn't much help, because walking down the aisle was the scary part.

Every couple of steps I glanced from side to side just to double check that there weren't any people in the seats. There weren't, but the minute I took my eyes off the seats it was like I could hear them breathing.

"Eeeeeeee!"

My knees went buttery like they were going to fall off. I hung onto the flashlight like it was a railing. The light in the dressing room came back on. It flickered a couple of times, then it was gone. I felt awful little things walking all over me.

Then the strangest thing of all happened. This weird wind blew out of the dressing room and across the stage. It was coming right at us.

I know you can't see wind, but we did. I was looking at the open dressing room door. The only light in the whole place was what came from my flashlight and what filtered in through some skinny windows way up at the top of the auditorium walls. They're so dirty that the light that gets in through them looks like smoke.

But the wind didn't look like smoke. It didn't *look* like anything. But we could see it. It came across the stage in a little puff and then floated down the aisle toward us. Nobody could move. It felt like when it got to you it would suck you up in it and you'd disappear. That's the way I felt, at least.

The wind blew right by. I could feel it. It was colder than air conditioning on a really hot day.

"Whooooof!"

Dell sucked in a loud breath when the cold hit. I would have too, but my teeth were chattering so that I couldn't open my mouth. It was like standing in a tank of ice water up to my neck.

Then it was gone. The wind and the cold just went away. It was so quick that if we hadn't been paying attention, it would have been like somebody opening and closing a refrigerator door in front of us so fast that we couldn't even get a glimpse inside.

"What was *that*?"

Nobody knew.

Tyler was standing right next to me.

"Point the flashlight up there, Andy," he said.

I pointed, but my arm was shaking so badly that the little circle of light bounced around the stage like a white rubber ball. Tyler grabbed my arm to steady it. The light slowed down some, but it didn't stop shaking.

We all watched as the ball moved slowly across the stage. It stopped at the dressing room door.

The door was closed.

"Maybe the wind blew it shut," Tricia said.

"What wind?" Sandy asked.

"The wind that came by here a sec ago and nearly froze me," Dell said. He was really shaking. "Didn't you guys feel it?"

Sure we had, but things were happening so fast around there that nobody had time to mention one weird thing before another one happened.

"Sure, we felt it," we all said.

Dell looked relieved. "Maybe we should go back to Walgreen's and figure out what to do next," he said.

That sounded like a pretty good idea to me, but I didn't say anything. I wish I had because just then Tyler came up with an idea.

"If we leave we'll miss our chance to find out what's going on," he said. "This is a chance of a lifetime."

"For what?" I asked him. "To disappear in here or something? The chance I want for my lifetime is to make it longer, not shorter."

Tyler shook his head. "Don't be so dramatic, Andy," he said like he was scolding me. "How are we supposed to disappear?"

"That's what I don't want to hang around to find out," I said.

"I'll buy Pepsis for everybody if we go over to Walgreen's to talk about this," Dell said.

That's when I knew how serious things were. Dell holds onto his money so tightly that when he's forced to spend some you think Lincoln'll squirt off the sides of his pennies like seeds out of a grape.

"We just had one," Tyler said. He took the flashlight from me. "I'm going up there. If you guys aren't interested in finding out what all these lights and noises and cold winds are all about, that's o.k. with me. You can stay here, but I'm going."

Well, Tyler is all right. He's a scientist type, if you know what I mean. He's a good friend, too. None of us would abandon him. But I did notice that his feet weren't moving toward the stage any faster than Dell's or mine. Which means they were still glued to the floor like everybody else's.

"I'll go with you, Tyler."

Tricia! She's quiet most of the time. Why'd she pick a time like that to say something? But, since she's the smallest, it meant everybody had to go.

We inched down the aisle very slowly. Tyler kept the flashlight on the closed dressing room door. "I'll hold the light and you open the door," he said to me when we got on the stage.

When Tyler said that I knew right away why he gets such good grades. He's smart. The reason he took the flashlight away from me was so my hands would be free to open the door.

I listened at the door. There wasn't a trace of the sound from inside. I couldn't feel any cold either. I started to feel pretty good. It was like when you get home late and you think your house is empty and you don't want to go in because you'll be alone. And then you hear everyone talking in the kitchen so you go in. It's a relief is what I mean.

I grabbed the handle and turned it. "Sure, I'll open it," I said. The scared feeling was completely gone.

I pulled open the door. Tyler shot the light inside right away. He worked it around the room like he was painting the wall with it. It was empty.

We went in—me first, as usual.

Tyler messed around with the light switch. The light went on.

"Loose connection," he said. "That's a fire hazard. We better tell Sparky when we go back down."

"I'll go," Dell said.

Nobody paid any attention to him.

Tyler was like his old self. He was acting like nothing strange had happened. He turned out the flashlight and sat down at the make-up table that was against one wall. It was covered with dust like everything else, but he didn't mind.

"Did your dad ever tell you anything about this place, Dell?" Tyler asked.

Dell looked at him with kind of a "what do you mean" look.

27

"What do you mean?" Dell asked.

"Well, he's the mayor and everything. I thought maybe he knows something about the opera house."

Dell puffed up his chest. "Sure he does," he said. We all waited for Dell to say something, but he didn't.

"Well, what did he say?" Tricia asked.

Dell mumbled and shuffled around in the dust. "All he said was that we could use the place for a club if we cleaned it up."

That wasn't much help from the mayor, that's for sure.

Sandy sat down cross-legged on the floor. She put her hand on her chin. "Did he ever say anything about weird noises?"

"No," Dell said.

"What about flickering lights?"

"Uh-uh."

"Cold wind?"

"Nope."

"Anything unusual?"

Dell didn't like being the one getting all the questions. "Look, you guys," he said, "my dad never told me anything about this creepy, jerky old place. I'm getting sick of it if you'd like to know. I mean, how'm I supposed to know any more about this stupid opera house than you are?"

We all felt a little bad that Dell was getting upset. But we really wanted to know what was going on. It was worth the try, I guess.

"I'm sorry, Dell," Sandy started to say, then she stopped. She was doodling in the dust on the floor with her finger. She stared at the floor. She had drawn a perfect circle in the dust. And pressed in the dust in the middle of the circle was a U-shaped mark that was twice as big as the palm of her hand. We all saw it.

Tyler kneeled down for a closer look.

"What's that?" he asked.

"I don't know," Sandy replied. "I was just drawing circles and I noticed this mark, that's all."

Tricia pointed her sneaker toe at the mark in the circle. "You mean you guys don't know what that is?" she asked.

Dell moved a couple of steps toward the door. Sandy, Tyler and I all shook our heads. "No," we said. "What is it?"

"It's a horseshoe print," Tricia said as plainly as if she were pointing at Dell's dog and saying it was a dog. "What did you think it was?"

When Tricia said "horseshoe," all the goose bumps I'd ever had in my life came back all at once, because that's exactly what the mark in the dust was. It was a perfect print of a horseshoe. It was pressed in the dust as plainly as a design you press into clay.

"Eeeeeeee!"

The noise came from inside the room. We all knew what it was this time. It was a horse!

FIRE!

All of a sudden there was another noise. It was a shriek that sounded like a tornado roaring through the place. I thought the building was blowing up or something.

Dell shot out the door like he was on roller skates. Nobody waited around to see if he was coming back. We all took off.

We dashed out the dressing room door and jumped off the stage. We tore up the aisle and out the door at the back of the auditorium.

About the time we got to the door, the noise started to die down. That was the first we could tell what it was.

"It's only the fire siren, you guys," I hollered. But the others were already out the door. I ran after them.

"Hey, you guys," I hollered again. "It's the fire siren!"

Dell was out of sight. Tricia, Sandy and Tyler were by the outside door ready to bail out. They stopped. By then the siren was just making a long "ooooooo" kind of sound as it died out.

Dell was outside. "It's only the fire siren," he hollered through the door.

We went outside. Dell was standing there with his hand on the railing like he was just waiting around. He was trying to act like nothing unusual was going on.

"Let's go down to the fire hall and see where the fire is," he said. That sounded pretty good to me. I wasn't particularly interested in hanging around inside the opera house. Not since we heard that other sound.

Whenever there's a fire in our town you call the fire department number on the phone. Sparky is the one that takes the call. He's the one who blows the siren. Then he starts the trucks so that when the volunteers get there, they're ready to roll.

If the fire is a big one, Sparky starts the big

LaFrance. If it's just a little one or a brush fire, he starts the little truck.

In about three minutes the first volunteer firemen show up. Usually they're halfway to the fire five minutes after the whistle blows. My dad says they're really good. But he's not a member.

Sparky usually rides to the fires in the passenger seat of whichever truck goes. He's too old to drive anymore. He helps out by talking on the two-way radios and things.

We got down to Main Street about the time the first firemen showed up. One was Mr. Crispin who runs the Big C gas station down at the end of Main Street by the railroad tracks.

The firehouse doors were already open. The big old LaFrance was roaring. We stayed out of the way, just around the edge of the door.

Then the little truck started up.

"It must be a big fire," Sandy said. She stuck her head around the doorway and looked in. "Sparky's going to drive the little truck!" she shouted.

Mr. Crispin was behind the wheel of the big red LaFrance when it came growling out the front door on those big black tires. It doesn't have any mufflers, so it really makes a racket.

Sid Blanchard, who works at Penney's, and Mr. Corbett from Sandy's dad's hardware store, came running down the street and jumped on the LaFrance while it was moving. A couple of other men grabbed onto the back before it was going too fast. Anybody else would just have to catch a ride on the little truck or drive to the fire in his own car.

The little truck burned rubber and shot out the door like it came off a catapult. Its siren was whooping like on tv and Sparky was twisting that steering wheel like he was trying to unscrew it. You should have seen the look on everybody's face who jumped out of the way on the street when they saw it was old Sparky driving that thing. I never knew Sparky could drive, but he sure got that little red truck out of there in a hurry.

The fire hall was empty once the trucks were gone. It was real quiet and kind of eerie inside.

Dell went in. Since his dad's the mayor, he gets to act special sometimes. You don't mind, because when you're with him people don't tell you not to do things like going into the fire hall when nobody's there.

"Come on in, you guys," he said.

We did.

Dell walked to the back of the station. There are a bunch of old ladders on one wall and on the other there are about a dozen black and yellow firemen's coats with matching hats on hooks above them. The coats are old and cracked. The firemen nowadays have new stuff that they keep with them. They get fire messages on radios that they have so they go straight to the fire. I guess the old coats and hats are for memories or something.

"Look at that, you guys!" Dell shouted.

He was pointing at the blackboard where they write where the fire is so that anybody who gets there late will know where to go in case he didn't hear it on his radio.

"Mooney's barn!" Dell said. It was scribbled in big white letters across the blackboard.

"Holy cow!" Tyler said. "The fire's at Mooney's barn!"

"No wonder everybody got out of here so fast," Tricia said.

"That's why Sparky was driving, I bet," Sandy added.

We all looked at one another. Mooney's is the biggest barn in the whole county.

"Let's get out there!" Dell said. He was really excited. We all were.

"Let's get our bikes," I hollered.

We started running for the door. Then all of a sudden a noise worse than the siren stopped us in our tracks.

"EEEeeeeeeeeeee!"

We all looked straight up to the ceiling like we could see right through it.

"It *is* a horse!" Tricia exclaimed.

And then, just to prove it, we heard the other sound again.

Clump. . .clump. . .clump.

"Let's get out of here!" Dell hollered. He was already halfway down the street to the bike stand.

THE MYSTERIOUS EXPLOSION

Nobody said anything about the noise in the opera house on the ride out to Mooney's farm. I don't know if everybody else just forgot about it or what. I know I didn't. I didn't want to say anything because all I could think of were questions. And the questions sounded stupid. Like, "What's making that noise?" or, "How could there be a horse in the opera house?" Nobody else said anything, so I didn't either.

"There's the smoke," Tyler shouted. He was in the lead. He was pointing like crazy over the top of the trees at the edge of town along Route 12.

A tower of really black smoke was boiling up from behind the trees. I never saw so much smoke in my life. It looked like a picture of a volcano erupting.

We really started cooking down the road. Even Tricia kept up and she's only got a three-speed.

"That's the most smoke I've ever seen in my life," Tyler hollered.

"The whole farm must be burning."

"Maybe an airliner crashed or something."

"It looks like a volcano."

When we got to the corner of Route 12 and Old Town Road that leads to the farm, we could see the whole thing. There's a thick grove of trees that blocks most of the buildings, but you can see the silos and the top of the barn.

But there wasn't any top of the barn. All there was was smoke. "Holy cow! The whole barn's on fire!" Dell hollered.

We skidded to a stop at the side of the road. We had to be on the lookout for all the cars that were roaring down the road to the fire.

Not everyone was a volunteer fireman—Mrs. Douglas, for example. The back of her car was filled with groceries and Douga Douga, who is kind of weird, was sitting in the front seat.

Douga Douga hollered something at us when

they went by. He had this dumb grin on his face. Knowing Douga Douga, he probably said something like, "Hey, the barn's on fire." He's not known for being the first one to put his hand up in class, if you know what I mean.

The farmyard was jammed with people and cars by the time we got there. It looked like everybody in town was there.

The barn was out of sight. Flames and smoke were pouring straight out of the ground, it seemed. If I didn't know there was a barn there, I would have said it was a volcano.

"Everyone stay clear of the firemen!"

Chief Ordway was standing on the hood of the police cruiser. He had a bull horn and was waving it at everyone to get back.

Firemen were running through the crowd. You couldn't tell who was who because they didn't have time to put on their coats and hats like they usually do when they go to a fire.

"This is the biggest fire that ever happened in Montville, I bet," Tyler said. You'd have to be from out of town not to know that.

Skeeter Hanson came over to where we were standing with our bikes. We didn't dare put them down because there were so many people wandering around they'd get trampled or driven over or something.

"The jimmy blew up," Skeeter said. He was covered with soot. Usually he's got red hair and freckles, but you couldn't tell.

Skeeter's dad drives a truck, so Skeeter's crazy about trucks. The jimmy is what he calls Mr. Mooney's big truck. I think it's because it's short for GM, but I'm not sure. Trucks are o.k., but I don't go around making up nicknames for them. I want to fly jets when I grow up, so trucks don't interest me.

"How'd it happen?" Tyler asked Skeeter.

"Don't know," Skeeter said. "But I was the first one here. My mom was taking me and my sister up to the town pool. We came around the corner off Main Street and Katy says, 'There's smoke up at Mooney's,' and by the time we got to Old Town Road the sky was full of cinders and soot.

"We got here before the fire trucks even. Did you see old Sparky driving the little truck? I did. I was standing right down there by the chicken house when he come in on two wheels. Nobody ever said he could drive. I bet he don't even have a license."

Skeeter was so excited he couldn't stand still.

"I was the only one who saw the jimmy blow. There wasn't anybody else here. I seen it through the window of the barn. It was there one sec and then, pkchewwwww, it went off like it was a bomb."

Then his face got sour looking.

"There was a horse in there, too," he said. He sounded sad.

I looked at Tyler and Tyler looked at me. "Mr.

Mooney doesn't have any horses," I said.

Skeeter shook his head from side to side.

"Well, he sure don't now," he said.

"I mean he never did," I said. "That barn's been empty except for storing stuff since they shut down the dairy.

I remembered exactly when that was, because it was when the milk we get at school stopped coming in containers that said "Mooney's Dairy" on them. It was two years ago at least.

"It's two years at least," I said, "And even then they didn't have horses. Just dairy cows."

Skeeter shrugged his shoulders. "Beats me. All I know is I heard a horse in there."

Tyler grabbed me by the arm just before I was going to say something else to Skeeter.

"What did it sound like?" he asked Skeeter.

Skeeter looked at Tyler like he was stupid. "Like a horse," he said.

"I mean, what did the *sound* sound like?"

Skeeter scratched his head. Some dead cinders from the fire fell out. He was watching the fire and his attention was kind of scattered like he'd rather watch the firemen and everything instead of talk to us.

"It just sounded like a horse," he said. "What do you expect a horse to sound like? A chicken?"

Tricia stepped right in front of Skeeter's face. She's smaller than he is, but when Tricia does that to you you can't miss her.

"We want to know exactly what kind of a

sound you heard," she said. She may be little but she sure knows how to get her point across.

Skeeter's eyes got cloudy the way people's do when they're half sleeping in class or when they're trying to think too hard.

"Well?"

"I'm thinking."

Just then the ground shook like an earthquake. A big ball of flames shot up into the air. That was the end of the barn.

Skeeter got distracted. Tricia had to remind him of the question. We were all waiting.

"I bet you can't imitate the sound you heard," Tricia said.

"I bet I can." Skeeter grinned. His face was so black from soot that his teeth looked like they were made out of snow. He squinted his eyes tightly and put one hand to his mouth. His fist was open so it was hollow. He made a high-pitched sound into his hand.

"Heeeeeeeeeeee," he went.

Sandy, Tricia, Dell, Tyler and I all shivered. We knew the sound Skeeter was making. We had heard it before. It was the exact sound we heard at the opera house.

"Oh, yeah," Skeeter said as he started back to the edge of the crowd that was the closest Chief Ordway let anybody get to the fire. "I know it was a horse because I could hear it stomping around in its stall. It went *clump, clump, clump.*

Then the fire siren in town went off and it stopped."

Skeeter disappeared into the crowd.

I was getting used to it, but my arms and legs were all covered with goose bumps again.

MISSING EVIDENCE

On Sunday morning we went back out to Mooney's farm. There was still smoke coming from where the barn used to be. The silos were still standing. They looked like a couple of Martians. They've got these silver dome roofs that look like helmets and some pipes on their sides were all twisted and bent like skinny little arms.

The air smelled like acid. There were lots of people roaming around. They came from all over the county to see if the story of the fire was true.

That's not why we were there. We wanted to find out if what Skeeter said was true. He said there was a horse in the barn.

We asked Mr. Mooney's hired man, Willy Wilson. Willy is John Wilson's uncle. John's in our class.

"Nope," Willy said. "Been no livestock of any kind in the barn since he closed the dairy."

"Skeeter Hanson said he heard a horse," Tyler said, "just before the truck blew up."

Willy Wilson's eyes bugged big and white.

His face was grimy with soot like he'd been working a long time around the burned-out barn. He glared at us like we called him a name or something.

"Who said the truck blew up?" he asked. He looked scared. Or mean. It was hard to tell through all that soot.

"Somebody that got here before the firemen," Tyler said. "He saw it blow up. The one everybody calls the jimmy."

It was like somebody just told Willy that the sky was going to fall down. He looked at us with those big buggy white eyes for a sec like we did something awful. Then he spun around and ran to Mr. Mooney who was standing next to the pile of junk that used to be the barn. They started talking real fast. We couldn't hear anything because they were too far away, but it sure looked exciting.

"I wonder why he's so concerned that we know the truck blew up?" Tyler asked. I was thinking the same thing. The minute Tyler told Willy that we knew the truck blew up, Willy started acting really suspicious.

Mr. Mooney and Willy were still talking. Then Willy pointed at us like he was shooting a gun at us. Mr. Mooney walked over to us. He had on this big smile. He never smiles. He was acting like we were his old friends. The truth is that nobody in town is his friend because he always acts like he's better than everybody else.

"Well, I guess you kids came to see what's left of my barn," he said. He was still smiling. It didn't seem natural to me for somebody to be smiling the day after his barn burned down.

"Sort of," Tyler said.

"Willy tells me that one of you thought you heard my truck blow up," Mr. Mooney said. He was looking at each one of us really closely like he was examining a melon in the market to see if it was ripe.

We all shook our heads.

"It wasn't us," I said.

Mr. Mooney looked at me really hard. "Well, my hired man said it was and he knows better than to lie to me."

Mr. Mooney's smile was gone without a trace. If it wasn't daytime and all my friends weren't there and all the people weren't wandering around, I'd have jumped on my bike and gotten out of there so fast the paint would peel off.

Mr. Mooney is a big guy. He looked at us one by one. "Now, which one of you thinks you heard a truck blow up in my barn?"

None of us moved or said a word.

Mr. Mooney smiled again. This time it was kind of crooked like he had a seed stuck in his teeth. "That's just fine," he said, "because there wasn't any truck in the barn in the first place." He looked each one of us straight in the eye like he was trying to burn a hole through us. "Now you kids get out of here. I sure wouldn't want any of you to get *hurt*."

He let that sink in for a minute. Then he turned around and went back to Willy Wilson. We rode down to the end of Old Town Road and parked our bikes. We made sure it was public property.

"Something really strange is going on if you ask me," Tyler said. "Did you see the way he looked at us?"

"And did you hear the way he said *'hurt'*?" Sandy added. "It was like he was saying we'd better get out of there or we'd *get* hurt."

"Why do you think we're sitting here instead of there?" Dell said. Dell was right. The only reason we left the farm is because Mr. Mooney scared us.

"I think there's something about that fire that he doesn't want anybody to know about," Tricia said. She'd been kind of quiet, like she was thinking. "It's something about the truck, if you ask me."

"There wasn't any truck."

Sandy said that and then just sat there on her knees waiting for someone to ask her what she meant by that.

"What do you mean, Sandy?"

Good old Tyler.

"I mean there wasn't a truck, because I looked."

We were all sitting in a circle around Sandy like she was a counselor at camp telling a story.

"While Tyler and Andy were talking to Willy Wilson, I went over to the barn. What's left of it, I should say. There wasn't a truck in there during the fire because there would have been a wreck in the debris. And there wasn't."

Sandy was right. I remember looking at the barn when we got there. There wasn't anything in the piles of smouldering boards and tumbled-down bricks that looked anything like a burned-out truck. All there was was a big pile of burned boards and those two big scorched silos standing there like Martian guards.

"You're right, Sandy," I said. "I didn't see a wrecked truck in there either. If a truck blew up in there we'd have seen something."

Tyler rubbed his chin. He was looking back up the road to the grove that hid Mooney's farm. You could still smell the acid in the air. "I think we should go back there and take a look," he said.

Dell sat up straight as if a turtle had bitten him.

"Go back there after what he said?" Dell exclaimed.

Tyler shook his head. "Not now," he said. "Tonight. When it's good and dark."

Dell was trying to talk, but he was swallowing so hard that nothing came out.

We agreed that we'd meet after supper. When it got dark we'd go back to the barn. Things were getting much too mysterious for all of us—even Dell.

THE GHOST

I don't know if I was glad about the moon or not. It was nearly full, so you could see pretty well even though it was late. That was fine by me because one thing I didn't want to do was to poke around Mooney's burned-down barn and not see if there was anybody else there. The trouble was, if I could see them, they could see me.

"Everybody have their flashlights?"

Tyler took charge of the expedition because it was his idea. Nobody minded. We hardly ever do. Usually the person who's best at something ends up leading anyway. I like outdoor sports, so when we go skiing or backpacking or canoeing I'm the one that organizes it. It's the same for the others. We don't argue a whole lot.

We stood around in the dark, down at the end of Old Town Road. We walked from town because it's not a good idea to ride bikes at night, even if they do have lights.

"We'll stay on the road all the way to the farm," Tyler said. "But if you see any lights from cars or anything, holler and hit the ditch."

I felt like I was in a war movie.

We started down the road toward the farm. The moon was bright enough to see without using our flashlights.

"Car!"

Everybody jumped into the ditch alongside the road. A car came out of the driveway from the farm, heading straight toward us.

We ducked. Tyler poked his head up for a sec just as the car went by.

"It's Mr. Mooney," he whispered.

We waited until the car turned off Old Town Road and headed for town before we climbed out of the ditch.

"Maybe there's nobody left at the farm now," Dell said. It sounded like he was making a wish.

"Maybe. Maybe not," Tyler said. "But don't take any chances. Stick together."

You couldn't have stuck us any closer together if you put a rope around us.

We got to the grove at the edge of the farm. Tyler clicked his light on for a sec. "Let's cut through the grove," he said. "That way nobody'll see us, just in case there is somebody at the house."

The house was dark. We went through the woods anyway.

"Hey! Look at this!"

Sandy was standing by the silos. Her light was pointing at the ground. Tyler and Tricia and I went over to see what she was looking at. I don't know where Dell was.

We all pointed our flashlights at the ground.

There were bulldozer tracks everywhere.

"They're bulldozing the junk from the fire," Tyler said.

The tracks led into a field close by. There was a big hole dug out there. The junk from the barn was piled up in the hole. It was nearly full.

Tyler climbed down into the hole. We shined our lights for him so he could see. He poked his own light around the charred boards and blackened bricks.

"Holy cow!" he hollered as if he stepped on a wet frog or something. "It's the jimmy!"

We all started running faster than we did out of the opera house on Saturday when the siren went off. Tyler came racing out of that hole like a drowned gopher. Dell was right in his way. Tyler crashed straight into him and they both fell down in a heap.

Tyler got up on his knees. "Let's get out of here," he hollered. "The jimmy's down there in the hole. It's all covered up like they're burying it. Mr. Mooney lied. Something is going on around here he doesn't want anybody to know about."

Dell stood up real slowly like he was waking up in the morning. He had a funny look on his face like he was dreaming.

"Didn't you hear what I said?" Tyler asked. "They're doing something out here that nobody is supposed to find out about."

"Yeah, sure," Dell said. He sounded like he was asleep.

"Then let's get out of here," Tyler said. He glanced over at the house just to make sure nobody was coming.

Tyler and Tricia and Sandy and me were ready to cut out of there, but Dell just stood there looking stupid.

"I saw the horse," he whispered.

"What?"

"I saw the horse."

I was getting to be such an expert at goose bumps I didn't even bother to look at the ones that started crawling up my legs and arms and back like ants when he said that. My throat went dry the way it does when you eat choke cherries. The only thing that was holding me up was my knees, which bowed together like two boards leaning against one another.

I knew which horse Dell meant. We all did.

"It's the horse from the opera house," Dell said so quietly it sounded like he was blowing air through a hollow plastic pipe. "It's over there."

His arm rose into the air like it was tied to a hot air balloon. He pointed with a limp finger at a light glowing softly behind a corner of the burned-out foundation. It was the same light we had seen in the dressing room at the opera house.

Nobody could move. We stared at the glow. It was like a cold fire was burning on the other side of the wall. The light was bluish and flickered a lot. It would get brighter and then dimmer. A couple of times it almost went out.

"EEEeeeeeeee!"

Nobody would believe this in a million years, but it's true. We all saw it. A horse stuck his head out from behind the wall. Then his neck. In a sec there was a whole horse standing in the moonlight looking right at us.

And we could see right through him!

A NEW MYSTERY

That was the last I saw of the other guys until we got back together the next morning at Tricia's house. Everybody took off out of that farmyard like they were pieces of a bomb going off. I didn't quit running until I got home. That's nearly three miles. If the gym coach hears about that he's going to wonder why I can run only two miles on the track at school. I should tell him why. As if he'd believe me—as if anybody would.

"Did you *see* it?"

That was a dumb question. Coming from Tyler made it twice as dumb. We had all seen the horse.

"Are you kidding?" I said. "You'd have to have had your head in a sleeping bag not to see it."

"Was it a ghost?"

My old friends, the creepy bumps, came back when Tricia asked that.

"It had to be," Sandy said. "I could see right through it."

I thought the things were going to crawl away with me.

"But ghosts aren't real," Tricia insisted.

"And neither is that burned-out jimmy truck down in that hole," I said, "because Mr. Mooney *said* so." I think she got my point.

"Whatever are you five talking about?"

Mrs. Springer came out on Tricia's back porch.

She had a plate of brownies in one hand and a pitcher of lemonade in the other. That's one of the reasons we like to meet at Tricia's house.

"Oh, nothing, Mom," Tricia said.

I would have said the same thing to my mom. What were we supposed to say? Something like, oh, we're just talking about the ghost horse we saw last night. That would be the end of the brownies right there. She'd start serving nuts. Get it?

"Well, it certainly sounds interesting, whatever 'nothing' is."

Mrs. Springer's pretty good about things like that. She kind of lets us do what we're doing. Some moms wouldn't. I know from experience.

When Mrs. Springer went back into the house Tyler leaned forward.

"I couldn't sleep last night," he whispered. "There's too much going on around here all of a sudden."

As if I slept a wink. I left the lights in my room on all night and left the door open too. And for good measure, I slept sitting up in my desk chair. If that horse was going to show up in my room, I wanted to see him before he saw me.

"What's in these brownies?" Dell asked.

I can't believe the guy sometimes. Here there's a ghost horse running around loose and a mystery about the burned-up jimmy truck, and he's curious about what's in the brownies.

"Honey and carob," Tricia said.

I should have known. They don't eat sugar and chocolate at Tricia's. Nothing but health food. The interesting thing is that it's usually pretty good.

"What I'm trying to figure out is why did we hear the horse at the opera house?" Tyler said.

"And see it," Sandy added.

Tyler turned to Sandy. "We didn't see it at the opera house. We only heard it."

"But we saw the light. That was the same. It had to be the horse."

"Nothing counts unless you can count it," Tyler said.

That must be one of his scientific expressions. I agreed with Sandy. The light in the dressing room had to be the horse.

"I think it was the horse, too," I said.

"But we need proof," Tyler said.

Everybody was listening.

"I say we go down to the opera house," Tyler said real secretly. "If we can get the horse to appear, then we know that whatever is going on has something to do with more than just the farm."

"What do you mean?" Dell asked. He was working his lips around the edge of another brownie.

"Look at it this way," Tyler answered. He tipped his head back and looked up at the sky like he was thinking hard. "We heard something at the opera house that sounded like a horse."

"Like a whinny and hoofbeats," Sandy said.

"Right," Tyler said.

"We also saw a light in the dressing room that was blue and hazy, just like the light from behind the wall at the farm just before the horse came out."

"Right," Tyler agreed. "So I think it's reasonable to assume that there's some kind of connection between the opera house and

Mooney's farm."

"Don't forget the burned-up jimmy and that Mr. Mooney lied and said it wasn't burned up. We saw it, too."

Now everybody was calling a truck by a nickname.

"Right," Tyler said. "But that's as much as we know for certain. We don't know for sure if the noise and light at the opera house was the horse we saw at the farm."

"Aw, come on, Tyler," I said. "What else could it be? There can't be two ghost horses in one town." I mean, one was enough for me.

"I don't think so either," Tyler said. "But we have to make sure before we jump to conclusions."

"So we go down to the opera house and see if we can get the horse to come out? Is that what you mean?" I asked. "How do we do that? Offer it some ghost sugar cubes or a ghost carrot?"

Everybody looked at me like I had peanut butter on my chin.

"Be serious, Andy."

I shrugged my shoulders. The whole idea of getting a ghost horse to show up wasn't my idea of a good vacation. But it was four against one.

"O.k." I said. "We go down there and see. But let's do it while there's still plenty of light." I checked the sun just to make sure it wasn't going to go down all of a sudden. It was still morning, so I guess it was safe.

THE GHOST RETURNS

"Well, good morning, me buckos."

Sparky was standing at the front of the fire house. He had on a clean shirt and he was wearing a fireman's jacket with a big "MVFD" stitched in a half circle on the back. It stood for "Montville Volunteer Fire Department." People were waving at him as they walked by. It must have been because he had driven the little truck to the fire.

"Hi, Sparky," we said.

"You kids see the fire on Saturday?"

Now I knew he was standing outside on the street to show off. Everybody in town saw the fire.

"What fire?" I asked.

Sparky looked at me like I just said I'd never heard of Montville. "Why, the fire out to Mooney's," he said with a surprised look on his face. "Lord! The whole barn burned down right to the ground."

He looked me square in the eye. "Had to drive the truck myself," he said. He was puffing up inside that jacket like he was blowing up balloons in it. I noticed he didn't say if it was the little truck or the big La France.

"Gee!" I said.

That got old Sparky puffing up so fat I really did think he was filling up balloons under his jacket. That scared me, so I decided not to tease him any more. If he blew up, it would be my fault.

"Yes sir," he said. "When that call come through, why, I knew it was now or never, so I jumped on that old truck and wheeled her out the door near 60."

Sparky stopped his story to wave at someone across the street. Before he could start up again, Tyler asked him a question.

"Did the barn explode when you were there?"

Sparky jerked back like Tyler had stuck him in the eye with a stick.

"Explode? Lord, no! It was just a ball o' fire. Whole building was covered with flames like it was alive. Tarnation! That barn must've been dry as a dust ball to burn so fast. I never seen anything like it in my life. And that's near onto 75 years, don't you know."

"Were there any animals in the barn, Sparky?" I asked.

"Yes sir, come October ol' Spark'll be 75 years old. Huh?" he asked, like my question just arrived slow delivery or something. "Animals? Nope. There ain't been any animals in that barn since they sold the dairy."

Which meant that if the ghost horse was real, which it was, it wasn't the ghost of anything that got killed in the fire. It was a ghost for another reason.

"We're going upstairs to the opera house," Tyler said. "If you hear any noise or anything, it's only us cleaning."

Sparky acted like he heard us, but he was already smiling and waving to everybody that walked by.

The auditorium and stage were just the way we left them on Saturday. The only thing different was the dressing room door. It was closed. I know it was open when we all tore out of there on Saturday.

"The door's closed," Dell whispered.

We tiptoed down the auditorium aisle toward the stage. Everybody kept his eyes glued on the door.

"Eeeeeee!"

"He's in there!" Sandy screeched.

"That's what I was afraid of," Dell whispered. He started tiptoeing back up the aisle.

"Come on, Dell," I said. "Either we all stay or nobody stays." I was hoping everybody would agree with the last part. But Dell came back.

We climbed onto the stage, staring at the closed door like it would fly open at any minute.

Clop, clop, clop.

We froze in the middle of the stage like statues. The door to the dressing room was creaking open. A light came through the open crack. It was the same blue light we saw before.

"Where's the broom?" Tyler whispered.

"In the dressing room," I said. I knew because I dropped it there on Saturday.

Tyler looked around the stage. "See if you can find something to push the door open with," he said.

I don't know how he gets guys to do things like that, but he does. Maybe I'm just meant to go through life being the one that pushes doors open and goes into spooky rooms first.

I found a cane at the back of the stage. It was a prop from the last play. It wasn't nearly as long as I wished. If I had had a choice I'd have gone

down to Montville Building Supply and gotten a 20-foot pole. Or a 40-foot one if they come that long.

I sneaked up to the dressing room door with the cane out in front of me like a sword. I don't know what I was supposed to do with it if something came out. But I was ready.

When I got close enough to the door to reach it with the cane, I gave it a push with the tip.

The door flew open.

A bright blue light inside nearly blinded me.

"What's in there?" Tyler asked.

"I can't tell," I said. I was rubbing my eyes.

"Eeeeeeee!"

I jumped backwards like I got hit in the stomach with a swing. The cane went flying over my head and landed 20 rows back in the auditorium.

It was the horse!

It came out of the dressing room right for me. It was throwing its head back and forth like chariot horses in history books do. It had a wild look in its face. You couldn't tell for sure what color it was underneath because of the bright light it gave off. Its mane was flying all over its neck like blue electricity and its tail looked like a Fourth of July fireworks fountain.

The horse was prancing. Its eyes flashed like it was scared. Its mouth was open wide and every once in a while it made a high-pitched scream that got the creepies crawling up and down me like I fell into a spider's nest.

The horse's hoofs clattered across the stage like somebody was beating on the floor with hammers. We could see right through him! We could see the dressing room right through the horse!

I couldn't move. I was shaking so hard my sneakers were squeaking on the floor.

The other guys just stood there staring up at the horse. Dell's mouth was open so wide you could have put a whole orange in it. Tricia was blinking so fast you couldn't tell if her eyes were open or shut. Sandy had a hold on Tyler's arm and was holding it up in front of her like a shield.

The horse pranced out onto the stage. It spun around a couple of times in that fake living room like it didn't know exactly where it was. Then it calmed down. It didn't exactly go to sleep, but it slowed down some.

It wandered toward the back of the stage. None of us could take our eyes off it. It wandered around like it was looking for something.

"It's the same horse from the farm!" Tyler said too loudly to suit me. "It's got a white blaze on its nose and white boots on three feet just like the one at the farm."

I shook my head in amazement. All I saw both times was a blue-white ghost horse, and here's my friend the scientist making observations.

"What's it doing here?"

Tricia was shaking her head in disbelief when the horse just walked straight through the canvas backdrop at the back of the stage and disappeared.

Tyler and I hurried to the backdrop. Tyler pulled it open where two sections came together. The blue light was still back there. The horse was walking around.

I stuck my head through the opening. Tyler was right. The horse had a white blaze on his snout. It had three feet that were white about halfway up to the knees. It looked like he was a chestnut color under the blue light. He was sniffing around. His nose was going up and down the back wall like there was something there. There was nothing that I could see except the brick wall in back.

Then it stopped. It nuzzled its nose against a part of the wall the way a horse does when it eats oats out of your hand. It got real calm like there was someone there. And then it started to fade. It just got dimmer and dimmer the way it does when you turn down the lights.

"It's gone!"

Tyler was shaking his head like he had a fly on the end of his nose. My eyes were watering because I had held them open so long. I didn't dare blink as long as the horse was there.

There wasn't a trace left of him.

Tyler hurried over to the place along the wall where the horse was.

"Come here, you guys," he said.

I was so relieved that my feet and legs still worked that I would have gone anywhere.

Tyler was rubbing the wall with one hand.

"Feel this," he said.

I put my palms on the wall and wiped them over the bricks the way Tyler did.

"What about it?" I asked.

"Can you feel the difference?"

All I could feel was cold bricks.

Tyler grabbed my hands and pressed them hard against the wall.

"Feel the difference?" he said. Then he moved my hands about a foot to one side.

There was a difference. I could feel it. Part of the wall was uneven, like it was built at a different time than the rest.

Dell turned on the lights. I think we all felt a lot better.

You could see the difference in the wall. A small section of bricks was different than the rest.

"A window!" Tyler exclaimed. "Look! There used to be a window here."

Sandy was studying another part of the wall. "Not only that," she said. "There was a door back here too. A big one."

"Let's ask Sparky," Dell said.

It was an excellent idea. And it also gave us a chance to get out of that spooky opera house.

A STRANGE ENVELOPE

"Why, of course there was a door to the alley," Sparky said. He was leaning back in his chair, which he had moved to the front of the fire house so people could see him better. "How else were they supposed to get the horses to their stalls?"

When Sparky said "horses" I thought I was going to faint.

"*What* horses?" Sandy gasped.

"Why, the fire horses," Sparky said, like it was something we were supposed to know. "What other kind of horses live in a fire station?"

Sparky rubbed the top of his head.

"Years ago when I was just a boy, before they built the opera house, the upstairs was a barn for the fire horses. There were three of them," Sparky said. "Used to pull the old steam engine." He pointed to a dusty picture hanging on the wall near the old-fashioned coats and fire hats. "I'll show you," he said.

Sparky wiped off the picture with his sleeve. "There they are," he said. "Smokey, Chief and Blaze." He was puffing up again as if they were his horses.

"Which one is Blaze?" Tyler asked. He was so excited he could hardly talk.

"Why, this one right here," Sparky said. He pointed to a big chestnut stallion standing between a white horse and a gray horse. The stallion had a bright white blaze on its snout. Three of its feet had white boots that went nearly to its knees. It was the horse we saw upstairs in the opera house, and the same one we saw at Mooney's farm. It was the ghost horse.

"The horses came from the Mooney farm, didn't they, Sparky?" I asked.

Sparky looked at me really puzzled. "Why, how'd you know that?" he asked.

"I'm not sure," I said. "I just know." And that was the truth.

I went back up to the opera house with the other guys.

"Blaze is trying to tell us something," Tricia said. "That's why he showed up here and at the farm."

"But what? And why did he go to that bricked-up window?" Tyler asked.

"Ghosts never appear unless there's a reason," Sandy said. "All the ghost books I've ever read say that. There's always a buried treasure or a murderer who didn't get caught and things like that."

Sandy was right. All the ghost books I've read say the same thing.

"Do you think there's something in the window?" Dell asked. "Like a buried treasure or something?"

"There could be," Tyler said. "I say we go inside and find out." In about ten minutes we found what we were looking for.

"Look at this, you guys!"

Sandy had her hand on one of the bricks that filled in the hole where the window used to be. Scratched in it was a big "X."

Dell was so nervous when I started digging the brick out of the wall that he couldn't watch.

"What'll I tell my dad?" he said. "We're tearing down the whole opera house."

"We'll put it back," Tyler said.

The brick came loose. I tugged at it. It wiggled the way a tooth does when it's ready to come out.

"You're pulling down the whole wall," Dell said.

The brick was stuck. Tyler got his fingers in there with mine and we pulled. The brick popped out like a cork and smashed on the floor.

"It's hollow!" Tricia shouted.

The brick lay in a hundred pieces like a broken Christmas tree ball. It was a fake brick. And lying in the broken pieces was a long, thin envelope made out of lead.

WHAT'S GOING ON?

The envelope was about as big as a long envelope you buy at the store. It looked like someone made it by folding over a thin sheet of lead and soldering the edges closed. Whatever was inside would be protected forever.

Tyler held the gray envelope to the light. "There's writing on it," he said.

Scratched on one side were some wiggly words which said, "To the Town of Montville."

"I don't think we should open it," Dell said. "It's to the whole town."

"Let's take it to your dad," Tricia said.

Mr. Shaw wasn't in his office. There was only Miss Saybelle, his secretary.

"The mayor is having lunch with Mr. Mooney," Miss Saybelle said. "They're at Stamson's Restaurant. They'll be busy for at least two hours. Mr. Mooney is selling his farm to the town and. . ."

Miss Saybelle put her fingers over her lips like she burned them. "Oh!" she said, "I wasn't supposed to tell anyone."

We took off for the restaurant.

"They're sitting in the back," Tricia whispered after she walked in and looked around like she was looking for her mom or something.

"Then it must be true," Sandy said.

"But why is Mr. Mooney selling his farm to the town?" Tyler wondered out loud.

"And just after the barn burned down?" Dell added.

"Maybe it's a fire sale," I said.

Nobody laughed. They never do.

"Do you think there's any connection?" Sandy asked.

"There has to be," Tricia said.

"Then let's go back out to the farm and see if we can find any clues," Tyler said. "There's something really fishy going on, if you ask me."

We all agreed. I mean, when there's a ghost horse that keeps showing up and a bad fire and Mr. Mooney and Willy Wilson lying about the jimmy truck burning up, well, you don't have to be Einstein to figure out that something really weird is going on.

TAKEN PRISONER

"What do you kids want?"

Willy Wilson jumped out from behind the silos next to where the barn used to be. There wasn't a trace of the barn left. Everything was bulldozed. Even the brick walls. The place looked like a new parking lot.

"We just came to see the barn," Sandy said.

"Well, there ain't no barn left, so you can just hightail it out of here," Willy said.

Willy never talked to us like that before. He was acting like he was a different person.

"We're not hurting anything," Tyler said.

Willy stared at each one of us. Then he saw the lead envelope tied onto Dell's bike carrier.

"What's that?" Willy asked.

"It's for my dad," Dell said.

"Oh, is that so?" Willy shot back. "We'll just take a look and see about that."

Dell jumped on his bike and was pedalling away before he hit the seat. Willy started after him, but it was no use.

Willy came back puffing like somebody tightened his belt too tight. His face was redder than the barn used to be.

"You kids get out of here and don't come

back," he hissed. "And don't you dare tell nobody about that jimmy either. It got sold two weeks ago."

We knew that was a lie. We knew the jimmy got burned up in the fire. And we knew where the wreck was.

"If it's sold, then what's that buried in the hole that's covered up back there?" Tricia said.

Oh, Christmas! I wanted to get out of there in a hurry. But Tricia just stuck her chin out at Willy.

"Wha?. . .there ain't. . .what hole you talkin' about?. . .there ain't no hole. . ."

Willy was stuttering so badly his teeth clicked.

"There was, but it's all covered up now," Tricia said. "And we know the jimmy's in there, because we saw it."

Double Christmas, I wished I was an ant.

Willy got white in the face. All the red disappeared like somebody pulled a plug somewhere. He tensed up like he didn't know what to do. Then, without warning he jumped at Tricia and grabbed her by the hair. He grabbed for me with his other hand but I jumped clear over my bike like I had grasshopper legs all of a sudden.

Tricia squirmed and kicked but she couldn't get loose.

"You let her go," Tyler hollered.

But Willy was acting like he was crazy. He dragged Tricia by the hair toward the silos.

"You kids got no right to come out here and get me in trouble," he wailed like he was going to cry or something. "I done everything Mr. Mooney told me to do. I loaded all of his daddy's papers and books and things on the jimmy just like he said. I hid the jimmy in the barn like he told me. I was goin' to take the papers out into the field and burn them like he said but the gas spilled and the whole thing caught fire in the barn before it was supposed to."

Willy was screaming at us. Tricia just stood there, too scared to move. Not that she could if she tried.

Willy pulled Tricia into the silo.

"Mr. Mooney promised me I could stay on at the farm after he sold it to the town," Willy screamed. "But now you ruined everything."

Willy and Tricia disappeared inside the dark silo.

"He's crazy," Dell said, screeching to a stop on his bike. "Did you see him come after me?"

"Never mind you," I hollered. "He's got Tricia prisoner in there." I pointed at the silo just as this ear-splitting scream came from the open doorway at the top.

Tricia was balanced on the ledge 60 feet off the ground with Willy teetering back and forth behind her like he was going to fall any minute. His hand was snarled tightly in her hair like he was holding onto a clump of straw.

If Willy fell, Tricia would fall too.

BLAZE RETURNS

I ran to the ladder on the side of the silo. Just before I started up I heard a noise from inside.

"*Eeeeee!*"

"Blaze!" I hollered.

Blaze was inside the silo. He was reared up on his hind legs. His head whipped back and forth and white foam blew from his nostrils like blue sparks. His eyes were wide and full of fire.

"Easy, boy!" I hollered. "It's o.k." It wasn't like Blaze was a ghost at all. It was just like he was a real horse.

Blaze settled down. He pawed the floor. It was like he knew something was really wrong.

"Come outside with me, Blaze," I said. "Let Willy see you. I'm going to tell him you'll haunt him if he doesn't let Tricia go."

Blaze shook his head like he understood. Tricia was screaming.

"Come on, Blaze," I said. "It's our only chance." I ran outside.

"Please, Blaze," I called. But the ground door to the silo was empty.

"Eeeeee!"

Blaze didn't need a door. He leaped straight out through the wall like it wasn't there.

"Hurry, Blaze," I hollered. "Follow me!" I ran around the side of the silo to where Willy could see us. Blaze was right behind me, snorting and pawing the air like he was wild.

The minute Willy saw us his eyes rolled back in his head like he was seeing things. "Mr. Mooney," he said like he was in a dream. I looked around. Mr. Mooney wasn't anywhere in sight.

"Mr. Mooney," Willy said again. He was staring straight at me. "I told your boy I didn't want to burn them papers, Mr. Mooney," Willy

wailed. "But that no good son of yours said if I didn't he'd fire me for good."

I was confused. Then it dawned on me. When Willy saw Blaze standing by my side, he thought I was old man Mooney, the father of the one who hollered at us and was going to sell the farm to the town.

Willy was teetering on the edge of the silo roof and holding onto Tricia's hair like it was a railing.

"Don't be mad at me, Mr. Mooney," Willy pleaded.

Willy was seeing things. I mean, he really was seeing things. Blaze was pawing the ground next to me like a real live horse.

I stood up as tall as I could.

"Willy Wilson," I hollered in as deep a voice as I could to imitate old Mr. Mooney. "You bring that girl down from there this instant." I was so scared I couldn't think of anything else to say.

But it worked.

"Yes sir, Mr. Mooney," Willy said. "I'll do just what you say. Just like I always did when I was working for you. Things'll be just like they used to be, won't they?"

Willy let go of Tricia's hair. The minute he did she grabbed the inside ladder and scooted down in less than a minute. She came tearing out the silo door so fast she nearly ran by us.

"Where's Willy?" Tyler asked.

"Inside," Tricia said. "He's really confused. He said he was going to get some oats for Blaze."

I had forgotten all about Blaze. I whirled around.

Blaze was gone.

"Where did he go?" I asked.

"Who?" Sandy said.

"Blaze! He was right here beside me."

All the others shook their heads like I was seeing things like poor old Willy.

"Blaze wasn't here," Dell said. "There was only you."

"But I. . ."

"Look!" Tricia exclaimed. She was staring at the ground.

Pressed into the fresh dirt was a perfect trail of hoofprints. They led straight out from the silo wall to where I was standing. They were identical to the hoofprint we saw in the dust in the opera house.

Tyler dropped to his knees for a closer look. He scraped away some dirt next to one of the prints. There was a piece of shiny metal underneath. He dug it up.

It was a brass name plate, the kind they put on stable doors. It was grimy and stained by smoke. Tyler brushed it off so it glistened in the sun. We all read the name.

"Blaze."

We were standing right over the place where Blaze's stable had been a long time ago.

THE MYSTERY IS SOLVED

We must have set a world's record for bike riding. We got to town almost as fast as a car, I bet.

"Is my dad still here?" Dell asked the waitress at Stamson's Restaurant.

She nodded. The mayor and Mr. Mooney were still at a table way in the back. There were some papers on the table. The mayor had a pen in his hand as if he were going to sign them.

Dell went ripping through the restaurant waving his hands and hollering. We were right behind him.

"Dad!" Dell shouted. "We've got something really important to tell you!"

We all gathered around the table. Dell told his dad what happened at the farm. He didn't mention Blaze, though. I thought that was smart.

The mayor was annoyed that we interrupted his meeting with Mr. Mooney. But when Dell mentioned the papers Willy said got burned in the barn fire, he got more interested. And Mr. Mooney got nervous.

"If you'd just sign the papers, Mr. Mayor," Mr. Mooney said. "As soon as you do you can spend the rest of the day with these young detectives." He said the word "detectives" like it was a sourball, and he looked so suspicious to me that I could almost see his picture on the wall at the post office.

"Just a moment, Mr. Mooney," the mayor said. He looked Dell straight in the eye.

"Now, son," he said. "You've raised some very serious allegations here. You're suggesting that Mr. Mooney's barn fire was set on purpose, and you're also suggesting that some important papers were deliberately burned in the fire."

Dell was nervous.

"Well, it's true, Dad," Dell said. "We saw the jimmy down in that hole ourselves. And Willy said he was supposed to burn all of old Mr.

Mooney's papers."

Mr. Mooney grinned. "Now, son," he said like he was our friend all of a sudden. "Everybody knows that Willy isn't quite all here." He tapped the side of his head and winked.

"But he never lied before the fire," I shouted. Mr. Shaw shook his head.

"Boys," he said. "These are such serious accusations that I'm going to have to study them much more closely. I'll meet with you in my office just as soon as Mr. Mooney and I finish this town business."

"Don't buy the farm!"

Tricia had such a look of surprise on her face that even she didn't believe she screamed that.

Everyone stared at her.

"Show them what we found in the hollow brick," she said.

Because of all the excitement, we had all forgotten about the lead envelope on Dell's bike. He ran out to get it. In a sec it was lying on the table.

"This is very interesting," Mr. Shaw said. He got a sharp knife from the waitress and started cutting a slit in the lead.

Hardly anyone dared breathe.

There was a piece of yellowed paper inside. Mr. Shaw read it out loud.

"Last Will and Testament of Earl B. Mooney, August 15, 1935.

"Why, this is your father's will, Mr. Mooney," the mayor said. Mr. Mooney, the son, grabbed the edge of the table with both hands so he wouldn't fall down.

The mayor kept on reading.

"My farm is hereby deeded to the Town of Montville to be preserved as a town park and open space for the enjoyment of all. Signed, Earl B. Mooney."

The mayor's face was grim. He looked young Mr. Mooney straight in the eye.

"You have no right to sell the farm to us," the mayor said. "It already belongs to the town."

Mr. Mooney stuffed his papers into his briefcase and hightailed it out of the restaurant like his stomach was on fire.

Later on in the mayor's office, Mr. Shaw asked us a bunch of questions.

"How did you find this will?" he said.

We all looked at one another.

"Er, we found it when we were cleaning the opera house," Tyler said, which was true.

"That's amazing," the mayor said. "The old man wanted to give his farm to the town. He must have suspected that his son might try to pull something."

"But why did they want to burn up all of old Mr. Mooney's papers?" Dell asked.

"I imagine the son figured that somewhere among them there was a will that gave the farm to the town," the mayor said.

"Or a letter or something that told where to find the real will in the hollow brick," Tricia said.

"So if he burned everything up, there wouldn't be any proof that there was a will," Sandy added.

The mayor smiled. "He almost got away with it," he said. "It's amazing that the old man realized way back then how precious open space lands are," he said. He sighed and looked out of his office window at Main Street. "All of us will benefit from this fine gift," he said. "We should all be grateful to old Mr. Mooney," he went on.

"I guess there's nobody who appreciates the value of open land more than someone who's lived on it all of his life."

Just then Tyler and Sandy and Tricia and Dell and I heard a noise from the direction of the old opera house.

"Eeeeeee!"

It wasn't very loud, but we heard it. We all smiled.

"Well, maybe there is someone that appreciates open land even more, Dad," Dell said.

The mayor had a puzzled expression on his face.

None of us tried to explain anything to make it go away. After all, it looked kind of like the mayor had just seen a ghost.

And in a way, I guess he had.